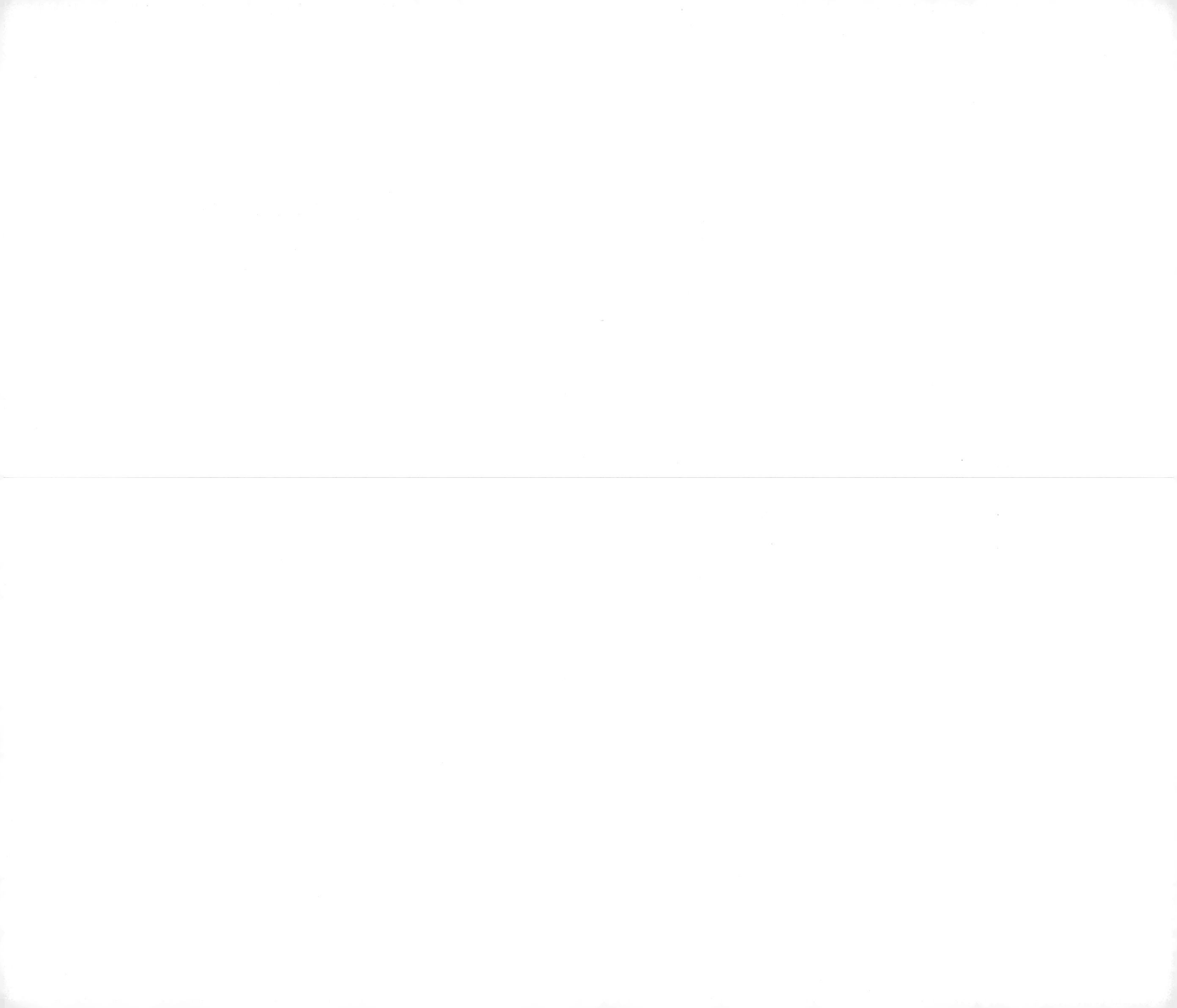

ZOO WORLD

# BLANCA AND ARUSHA:

## TALES OF TWO BIG CATS

BY GEORGEANNE IRVINE

SIMON & SCHUSTER BOOKS FOR YOUNG READERS

In memory of Anna, a special dog with a big heart; to Arusha, the most wonderful cheetah in the world; and with love to Kathy Marmack, a true friend of animals and to me.

ACKNOWLEDGMENTS

A special thanks to my cat-fancying friends, family, and colleagues: Kathy Marmack, Ron Gordon Garrison, Heidi Ensley, Suzanne Esterbrook, Carlee Robinson, Ken Kelley, JoAnn Thomas-Roemer, Becky Kier, Bobbie Cassidy, Pam Bauer, Ted Andrew, Bill Myers, Jeff Turnage, John Turner, Janet Larsen, Leah Bussell, Karen Killmar, Victoria Garrison, Laurie Krusinski, Dee Anne Traitel, Dorothy Irvine, Yvonne Miles, Phil Lemon, Adriane Ruggiero and Alan Benjamin—who are more fortunate than I because they don't sneeze in the company of cats.

PHOTO CREDITS

Jim Bacon: 30 left; Ron Gordon Garrison: front jacket left, back endpapers, 5, 6, 9, 10, 11, 12, 13, 14, 15, 16 lower, 17, 18, 19, 20, 21, 22, 23, 24, 25, 26, 27, 29, 31, 32, 33, 34 left, 35 top right, 36, 37, 38, 39, 40, 41, 43, 44; Ken Kelley: front jacket right, 28, 34 right, 35 lower; Georgeanne Irvine: 35 top left; Phil Lemon: 16 top left and right; Craig Racicot: 42; F.D. Schmidt: 30 right; Van Nostrand: 29.

SIMON & SCHUSTER
BOOKS FOR YOUNG READERS
An imprint of Simon & Schuster Children's Publishing Division
1230 Avenue of the Americas
New York, New York 10020

Designed by Edward Noriega
Manufactured in the United States of America

10 9 8 7 6 5 4 3 2 1

Library of Congress Cataloging-in-Publication Data

Irvine, Georgeanne.
Blanca and Arusha: tales of two big cats / by Georgeanne Irvine.
p. cm.—(Zoo world)
1. Blanca (Tiger)—Juvenile literature. 2. Arusha (Cheetah)—Juvenile literature. 3. Tigers—California—San Diego—Biography—Juvenile literature. 4. Cheetah—California—San Diego—Biography—Juvenile literature. 5. San Diego Zoo—Juvenile literature. [1. Blanca (Tiger) 2. Arusha (Cheetah) 3. Tigers. 4. Cheetah. 5. San Diego Zoo.] I. Title. II. Series: Irvine, Georgeanne. Zoo world.
QL737.C23I79 1995 636.8'9—dc20 93-47529 CIP AC
ISBN: 0-671-87191-9

# CONTENTS

# INTRODUCTION

**Kathy Marmack and Rimau, a clouded leopard**

AH-CHOO! Name any kind of cat—tabby, calico, Siamese, Persian, alley cat, fluff-ball cat, cheetah, leopard, tiger—and I'm allergic to it. But that has never stopped me from admiring and appreciating any cat's beauty, grace, hunting abilities, secretive and wily ways, moodiness, intelligence, and dignity.

During my sixteen years at the San Diego Zoo, animal trainer Kathy Marmack has shared with me her vast knowledge and insight on exotic big cats—from cheetahs and tigers to leopards and lions. Kathy, who has worked with almost every major big cat species, makes it very clear that exotic cats don't make good pets. The cats she has trained for educational shows—such as Blanca the white tiger and Arusha the cheetah—are featured in the following stories as goodwill ambassadors for their wild relatives.

Most of the exotic cats Kathy has raised were abandoned by their mothers or were sick as babies and in need of veterinary care. Many of them are placed into endangered species breeding programs when they are too big or mature to handle safely.

By introducing exotic cats to audiences at the San Diego Zoo, Kathy and her training staff share their concern that big cats are in big trouble. Many cat species are critically endangered because they're losing their habitats and being illegally hunted and killed for their fur and body parts.

I've seen firsthand some of the problems facing wild cats. In China, I was horrified to see Siberian tiger and snow leopard pelts hanging for sale in a gift shop even though the Chinese have strict laws protecting those species. The sales clerk told me each fur cost 900 U.S. dollars, but she was willing to bargain for less.

On the Indonesian island of Sumatra, I hiked through the smoldering remains of what was once a forest home to Sumatran tigers and other creatures. It looked as if a bomb had been dropped. In my journal I wrote, "It's quiet here except for the sound of a distant chain saw. This forest is dead!"

Exotic cats are precious to the world, and the world is waking up slowly to save them from extinction. International laws protect most wild

**A destroyed forest in Sumatra makes way for a settlement**

**A lioness lounges in Tanzania**

cats. Zoos and wildlife parks are breeding many rare species in captivity. Conservation groups and governments are working to stop poachers and the sale of exotic cat pelts. Some natural habitats are being set aside throughout the world as wildlife preserves. Scientists are also studying big cats to learn more about them. But as Kathy Marmack often asks, "Is enough being done?"

Only the future will tell.

*Georgeanne Irvine*

## BLANCA: A SPECIAL SNOWY WHITE TIGER

**Inspector Ted Andrew**

AN ORDINARY WHITE CAR crept slowly through the California freeway traffic on a hot August day in 1991, on its way to cross the United States border near San Diego, California, into Tijuana, Mexico.

Even though it was only mid-morning, U.S. Customs Inspector Ted Andrew had already surveyed several thousand vehicles as they passed into Mexico.

On occasion, Ted sent suspicious drivers to a second checkpoint for questioning and to have their vehicles searched. Ted was looking for things that were being smuggled out of the United States. Although U.S. Customs doesn't always check the cars crossing the border into Mexico, it was a special operation on that August 13th morning.

At 9:55 A.M., the white car approached Inspector Ted. He noticed nothing unusual about the two men in the front seat. As his eyes scanned the back seat, Ted was amazed to see a flash of white fur leaping wildly about. Even though the furry creature had been a blur, Ted knew that it was some kind of unusual and rare cat cub, maybe a leopard or tiger.

A surprised Inspector Ted escorted the car to the second checkpoint so that the occupants could be questioned. By now, the passenger was hiding the white cub under his feet on the car floor.

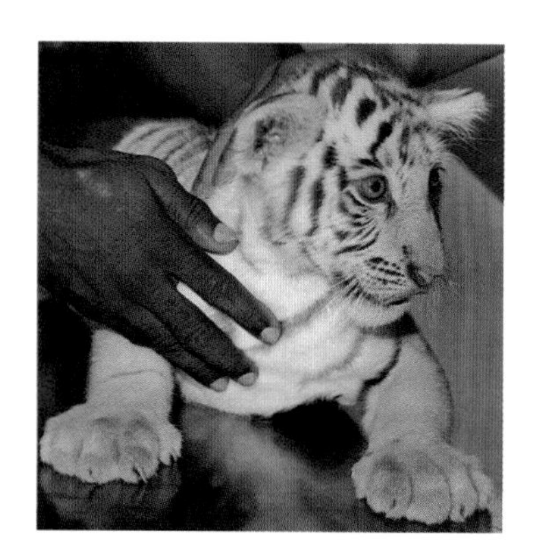

While the driver and passenger were questioned, Inspector Ted babysat the acrobatic cub. To Ted, the cub with its powder blue eyes, pale pink nose, and black stripes was one of the most adorable animals he had ever seen. The cub gnawed on Ted's arm as he placed the tiny cat in a cage.

Soon Bill Myers, a U.S. Fish and Wildlife Inspector, arrived to identify the frisky cat and decide what to do with it. Inspector Bill determined that the cat cub was a female white tiger. It was also an endangered species and very rare.

The two men who had been transporting the tiger were violating the law because they didn't have a permit to take an endangered species over the border. The cub was seized by U.S. Customs on behalf of the United States government.

The two men said that they didn't own the white tiger. They weren't arrested, but an investigation was started to find out who owned the cub. While the investigation took place—it would last many months—the nearby San Diego Zoo agreed to shelter the white tiger.

Inspector Bill delivered the rambunctious cub to the zoo hospital that afternoon. Keeper Jeff Turnage sat in a big cage with the spirited tiger so he could observe her closely and help the veterinarians determine her health and behavior. Watching wasn't easy when she pounced on him.

Jeff felt the cub was healthy, and figured that she had been hand-raised because she was so friendly. Any tiger baby who had been raised by its mother would be terrified of humans, and would demonstrate this by hissing and spitting at everyone.

The veterinarians examined the cub, vaccinated her against diseases, weighed her—she was fifteen pounds—and guessed that she was about ten weeks old. The zoo officials thought the white cat might be a Siberian/Bengal tiger mix.

Photos and a video of the special white tiger cub were taken. Soon her fuzzy, furry face was on television and in newspapers all across the United States.

Phone calls poured into the San Diego Zoo. Most people wanted to see the cub. Others wanted to name her after their pet cat or dog. Still others volunteered to adopt her.

So many people clamored to see the now-famous white tiger that after four days in the hospital she was moved to the San Diego Zoo's Children's Zoo nursery. There visitors could see her through two huge picture windows. The cub was named "Blanca," which means "white" in Spanish.

JoAnn Thomas-Roemer and Becky Kier were two of Blanca's nursery "mothers." JoAnn had raised tigers before, but never a rare white one.

When the nursery mothers cared for Blanca, they always chuffled to her first. Chuffles are how tigers greet each other, so Blanca felt comfortable with her human caretakers. To chuffle, JoAnn and Becky made the sound "foof" (which rhymes with "woof") repeatedly. Blanca always chuffled back.

Blanca was a big eater and loved mice, chicken, and a meat mixture called Nebraska Loaf. Mealtime was also playtime, though. Whenever a nursery mother entered her area with a pan of food, Blanca leaped across the room and wrapped her big furry paws around her caretaker's legs.

"No!" yelled each nursery mother, stomping her foot on the floor. Blanca usually let go, scurried across the room, and then pounced again. When Blanca finally settled down, it was time to eat.

Blanca loved chewing on gigantic bones and was very possessive of them. If anyone dared to come close to Blanca while she chomped on her bone,

**Kathy Marmack walks Blanca**

she'd growl at them. For fun Blanca also tore apart stuffed toy animals, splashed in a plastic swimming pool, and swung from a hanging tire.

The zoo visitors loved Blanca. The perky cub tried to pounce at kids through the windows, and then played hide-and-seek behind her sleeping box.

In early fall, when Blanca was three-and-a-half months old, she began going for walks (on a leash, of course) around the Children's Zoo. The exercise was important for Blanca's development, and it was good to expose her to new experiences.

Becky took Blanca for her very first walk. The striped cub was as wild as a tornado. She spent most of the walk jumping on Becky.

Because Blanca's manners didn't improve, zoo animal trainer Kathy Marmack was asked to help. Kathy, who was in charge of the zoo's Animal Chit-Chat Show, had lots of experience training tigers and other big cats.

At the nursery, Kathy greeted Blanca with a

chuffle as the wild cub pounced on her. But trainer Kathy had very strict cat rules: no biting, no grabbing, no bouncing.

When Blanca playfully bit Kathy's ankle and hung onto her leg with her sharp claws, Kathy firmly pushed Blanca away and harshly said, "No!" Blanca let go immediately.

Blanca was rewarded with a treat when she did something properly. Within a few days, the white tiger cub was walking more than she was jumping. She explored gardens of purple and pink flowers, splashed in puddles, and balanced on benches. If something scared Blanca, she nuzzled up to Kathy for security.

At the end of Blanca's thirty-minute walks, she chuffled contently as she went back to the nursery because she knew that a pan of food was waiting for her.

By November, five-month-old Blanca had outgrown her nursery pen. Kathy Marmack took charge of Blanca and moved the energetic fifty-pound tiger to a large enclosure near the Animal Chit-Chat Show creatures. Blanca's new neighbors included Arusha the cheetah, a timber wolf named Nocona, and Daphne, a six-foot-tall emu.

Blanca also met animal trainers Heidi, Suzanne, Alison, and Carlee, who would help Kathy take

care of her. Blanca was a little shy with them initially. For the first few days, the other trainers wore Kathy's turquoise jacket. Blanca was accustomed to the sight and smell of it, and therefore felt more relaxed with each new person.

Also in November, a businessman from Mexico, Mr. R., claimed that he was Blanca's owner. He said that Blanca had been born at his private zoo in Tijuana. According to Mr. R., without his knowledge, his nephew had taken the tiger into the United States so a relative could play with the cub. Mr. R.'s nephew didn't know he needed papers to

take Blanca out of and back into Mexico. Mr. R. wanted Blanca back.

The U.S. Attorney's office, which prosecutes federal crimes, felt differently. Assistant U.S. Attorney Leah Bussell spent several months gathering all the facts on Blanca's case. In January of 1992, Leah ruled that Mr. R. couldn't have Blanca back because he and his family had broken the strict laws that protect endangered species. In addition, Mr. R. was fined a whopping $25,000! Now it was up to U.S. Customs to decide on Blanca's future.

While U.S. Customs was determining Blanca's fate, the growing white tiger cub was trained to sit, stay, and lie down. Blanca was attached to her trainers and always tried to please them. It was important that Blanca minded the trainers because if she got too rough in her play, she might accidentally hurt them.

Blanca was rewarded with meatballs for good behavior. The meatballs were slightly frozen so Blanca wouldn't gobble them down too quickly. The cold meatballs also felt good in Blanca's mouth when she began cutting her permanent teeth.

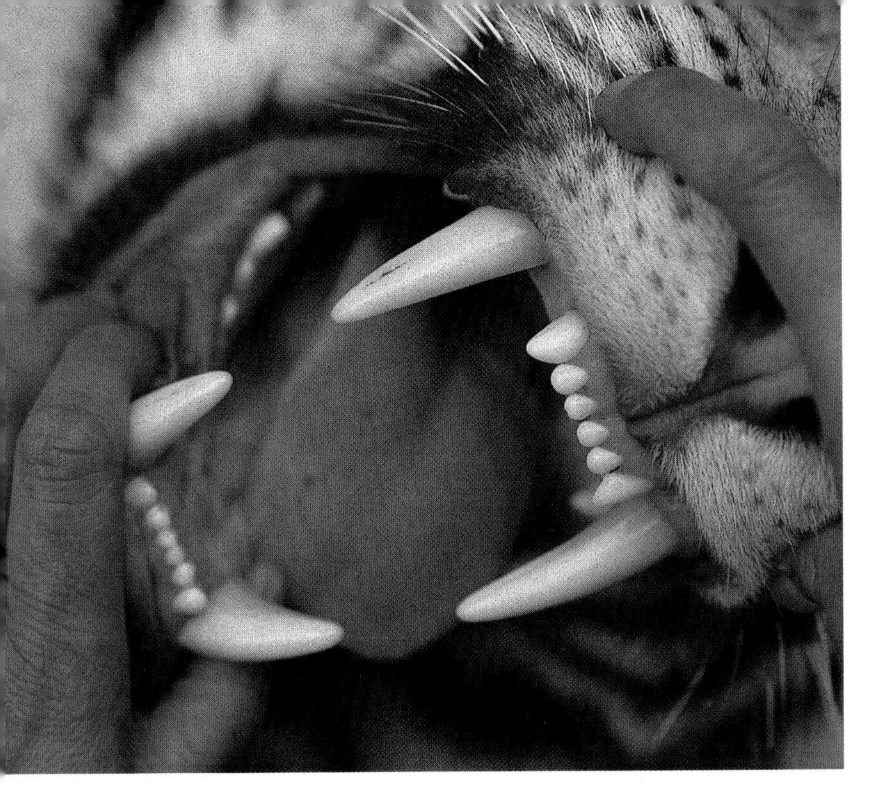

Because tigers have huge teeth, it really hurts when the adult teeth grow in.

Newspaper and television reporters still followed Blanca's story closely. Many media representatives came to the zoo on March 18, 1992, when U.S. Customs announced Blanca's permanent home.

Fifteen hundred excited school children hurried into the zoo's Wegeforth Bowl that day, along with many government and San Diego Zoo officials. Inspector Ted sat on stage with the president of the zoo and the U.S. Customs Commissioner from Washington, D.C., Carol Hallett.

Cameras clicked and video cameras whirred as Kathy Marmack walked nine-month-old Blanca onto the stage. When Commissioner Hallett stood next to Blanca and announced that the cub was to be adopted by the San Diego Zoo, the audience cheered and clapped. San Diego now had its very own white tiger.

"I am delighted to see that Blanca has found a home in San Diego in a zoo that is internationally famous for its care of animals," said Commissioner Hallett. "We at Customs understand the plight of endangered species and we know the importance of enforcing laws that protect them."

Now Blanca began starring in the Animal Chit-Chat Show with her human and animal friends.

Visitors came from everywhere to see the famous white tiger cub, who was growing bigger every day. The trainers chuffled at Blanca as they walked her on stage so she would feel calm and comfortable.

While Blanca prowled the stage, the audience learned from the trainers that all tigers are native to Asia, and are endangered species because their habitats are being destroyed. The audience also discovered that poachers have illegally killed many tigers for their gorgeous striped fur.

A white tiger, the trainers said, is white-and-black because of a recessive gene in that tiger's parents. Just as some people have brown eyes or blue eyes because of a gene, tigers can be white with black stripes or orange with black stripes. One concern, though, is that some people try to breed tigers that are closely related to each other, hoping the outcome will be a rare white cub. This is inhumane because the cubs can be born deformed or with health problems.

By December of 1992, one-and-a-half-year-old Blanca weighed 200 pounds. Even though she still minded and adored her trainers, Kathy was concerned that the big cub could accidentally injure someone because of her size and strength. It was time to move Blanca into the Tiger River enclosure in the main zoo. There she would have grassy hillsides for running and rolling, streams and pools for splashing, and big shade trees to nap under.

Before the big move, a zoo veterinarian examined Blanca. Kathy surveyed the Tiger River enclosure and met with the zoo-keepers who would be caring for Blanca. The media were notified that Blanca was graduating from the Animal Chit-Chat Show to her very own enclosure.

The day Blanca was moved to Tiger River the veterinarians put her to sleep for a short time so she could be carried to her new home in a large nylon web. Kathy thought about how she would miss walking her friend. She realized, however, that the move was in the best interest of everyone.

During her first week in Tiger River, Blanca stayed in a behind-the-scenes tiger bedroom area getting accustomed to the new sights, sounds, and smells. The Animal Chit-Chat trainers visited Blanca every day to help introduce her to the new keepers. They didn't get into the pen with her, but Blanca always greeted them with a chuffle.

During Blanca's first day on exhibit, trainers Kathy and Heidi stood nearby with the new

keepers to reassure the cub. As a clanging gate opened that led from Blanca's bedroom to the lush habitat of Tiger River, the young white tiger stepped into her new environment.

"What a good girl you are," Kathy said from outside the fence. "What do you think of your new home?"

With caution, Blanca crept down the grassy hillside to explore. A noisy dump truck dropped a load of dirt nearby. The racket scared Blanca and sent her scrambling up the hill toward the trainers. Kathy chuffled and fed her a small treat through the fence, which was all the encouragement Blanca needed to continue exploring.

Over the next few months, Blanca became more comfortable with her new surroundings and caretakers. Now, she is an adult tiger who prowls the grassy hillsides of her home, peering through bushes at zoo visitors. She splashes in the pools and naps under the trees. She gobbles up her meat meals, chews on bones, and even growls at her keepers.

But whenever Kathy Marmack visits Tiger River to admire Blanca, the big white cat bounds down the hillside to the edge of her enclosure and greets her old friend with a chuffle.

# ARUSHA AND ANNA: FOREVER FRIENDS

Kathy Marmack and Arusha

AN UNUSUAL AIRLINE PASSENGER sat with his furry face pressed against a cabin window, watching the scenery below, as his flight cruised from Oregon to San Diego, California.

Arusha, a three-month-old male cheetah cub, sat calmly on the lap of San Diego Zoo animal trainer Kathy Marmack, who was his travel companion. The hand-raised cat cub was a Halloween baby, born on October 31, 1980. He had been rejected by his mother at the Wildlife Safari Park in Winston, Oregon. Now he was heading to his new home in the San Diego Zoo, where he would star in the Animal Chit-Chat Show to help teach people about endangered species.

Initially, the well-behaved cub boarded the jet in a crate. But Arusha wanted out, so he chirped loudly, making some passengers think a bird was trapped between the lavatory walls. The pilot then gave special permission for Arusha to sit on Kathy's lap.

Arusha was named after a national park in Tanzania, a country in eastern Africa. There, wild cheetahs live in the dry, grassy savannahs. By nature, cheetahs aren't as ferocious as other big cats such as lions and leopards, especially if they have been raised by humans like Arusha was.

When they reached San Diego, Kathy introduced Arusha to trainers Carlee, Heidi, Amy, and Alison, who would help take care of the cheetah cub. Because Kathy and the trainers had other animals to care for as well, Kathy was concerned that Arusha might become lonely at times.

Kathy felt that Arusha needed an animal companion, but another cheetah was out of the question because the big cats are very rare and expensive. A zookeeper from Wildlife Safari Park suggested that Kathy get Arusha a dog as a lifelong friend. As crazy as the idea sounded, it made sense to Kathy. Cheetahs have dispositions that are quite dog-like, and they have about the same lifespan as dogs. Also, cheetahs have non-retractable claws just like dogs. These special claws act as cleats for cheetahs, which are the fastest runners of all land mammals. Cheetahs can run at speeds of up to seventy miles an hour for a short time.

The morning after Arusha arrived at the zoo, Kathy answered a newspaper ad selling an eight-month-old female golden retriever named Anna. The dog was the perfect age and breed. Golden retrievers are particularly friendly and patient.

A local family was selling Anna because she was too spunky for them. She had flunked obedience training twice, and had torn up the backyard rose bushes and new patio furniture. The family was more

Carlee, Arusha, and Anna

**Anna and Arusha meet Corky the harbor seal**

than happy to donate Anna to the San Diego Zoo.

When Arusha met Anna, he weighed only eleven pounds to Anna's forty-five pounds. Even though the tiny cheetah would grow up to be more than twice the dog's size, Anna was now four times bigger than Arusha.

During their first few hour-long meetings, Arusha hissed and swatted Anna on the nose. Anna didn't defend herself, though, which troubled Kathy. Soon Kathy realized that the dog was being extra-friendly to the small cat because Anna was trying to please the trainers, who were in the pen with them.

Kathy's new plan was for Arusha and Anna to be in a pen by themselves. The trainers would be able to observe their behavior from a distance. This time when Arusha hissed and swatted at Anna, the dog barked and defended herself. Arusha soon learned that Anna was in charge. Within a week and a half, the pair had bonded and become best friends. Arusha the cheetah was now dependent on Anna the dog, who was like a big sister to him.

Arusha and Anna were together all the time now. They snuggled during naps, played chase, swatted a soccer ball around, and went for long walks through the zoo with their trainers. Wherever Anna wandered, Arusha followed. Arusha felt secure and safe with Anna around.

In March of 1981, the cat and dog duo began appearing in the Animal Chit-Chat Show. When the unlikely pair bounded on stage with trainers Kathy and Carlee, the audience always gasped in amazement. Anna's and Arusha's show appearances usually ended with a big surprise: they were joined on stage by Corky, a young harbor seal. Corky was content to be near the cheetah and dog because Kathy fed him lots of fish. Anna liked

Corky because she was friendly with everybody. And, since Anna liked Corky, so did Arusha.

By the end of 1981, Arusha was bigger and stronger than Anna, but he didn't seem to notice. Anna was still the boss.

Anna had a real fondness for food, which sometimes caused problems. At mealtime, Anna often tried to gobble up Arusha's tasty meat dinners before the cheetah even had a chance to sniff them. Kathy's solution was to feed Arusha up on a platform, high above Anna's reach. The lanky cheetah was tall enough to jump on the platform, but Anna was much too short.

During their first year together, the trainers knew that Arusha was devoted to Anna. He constantly groomed her by licking her chest and forelegs with

his rough tongue, and stayed by her side. However, the trainers weren't sure that Anna was as dedicated to her cheetah friend. When her human caretakers were around, Anna always seemed more interested in them than in Arusha.

Then one day, Kathy and Carlee took Arusha to the zoo hospital to have a bad tooth removed. Arusha was very groggy from the anesthesia when the trainers returned him to the pen he shared with Anna. As first, Anna raced toward Kathy and Carlee. As soon as she spied groggy Arusha, though, Anna totally ignored her trainers and spent the rest of the day by her best friend's side. The trainers never doubted Anna's devotion to Arusha after that.

Over the years, Arusha and Anna became animal

goodwill ambassadors for the San Diego Zoo and shared many adventures. They traveled in a zoo van to school assembly programs, appeared on television shows, posed for magazine covers and calendars, met celebrities, and were special guests at fancy dinner parties and other events that raised money for conservation. They continued to appear in the Animal Chit-Chat Show, too.

Zoo visitors always remembered Arusha and Anna because it was unusual to see a 130-pound cheetah walking side by side with a 60-pound golden retriever.

Of the pair, Arusha was always the best behaved. At special events, Arusha usually relaxed on the

floor, purring loudly. He let people pet him on his head and back. He was a bit fussy about his feet and tail, though, and didn't like them to be touched.

Anna, on the other hand, seemed to get into mischief. Once in a while at the fancy parties, Anna jumped on guests' clothes with soiled paws or snatched food from the table when the trainers weren't looking. Anna was lovable, though, and everyone adored her.

If a new baby animal came to live at the Animal Chit-Chat area, the trainers often used Anna as a walking companion when they were leash-training the new arrival. Arusha was a one-dog cheetah, but Anna liked going for short walks with young Stosh the tiger, Boo the black leopard, or Nocona the timber wolf.

In 1990, Anna had some serious surgery at the zoo hospital to remove several tumors from her rear end. She and Arusha had been together for ten years but now they were apart for a day and night. This was the longest time that Arusha had been without Anna, and he chirped loudly because he missed her. The trainers sat for hours in Arusha's pen comforting him, hoping that Anna would recover soon.

Anna returned to Arusha with a T-shirt tied

around her rear end like a diaper to prevent her wound from getting dirty. Arusha purred loudly as he happily greeted his friend. He stood close to Anna while trainers Heidi and Alison put a big plastic collar around Anna's neck so she couldn't bite her T-shirt off.

Once Anna was fully recovered, the pair continued their zoo goodwill ambassador duties, only not quite as often. Ten years of age is old for a cheetah and a golden retriever. Kathy wanted to make sure that Arusha and Anna had plenty of time to rest.

In January of 1993, Arusha and Anna made their last appearance in the Animal Chit-Chat Show. Animal Chit-Chat was scheduled to be replaced with a new show called Wild Ones, in which Arusha and Anna would star instead.

But spunky Anna never made her Wild Ones debut, for she died of liver cancer in February.

There was not a dry eye in the zoo the day Anna died. Kathy, the other trainers, and all the people who had known Anna and Arusha over the years were devastated by the golden retriever's death. Everyone was very concerned about Arusha now that his lifelong friend was gone.

Arusha paced in his pen those first few days without Anna, even though the trainers sat with

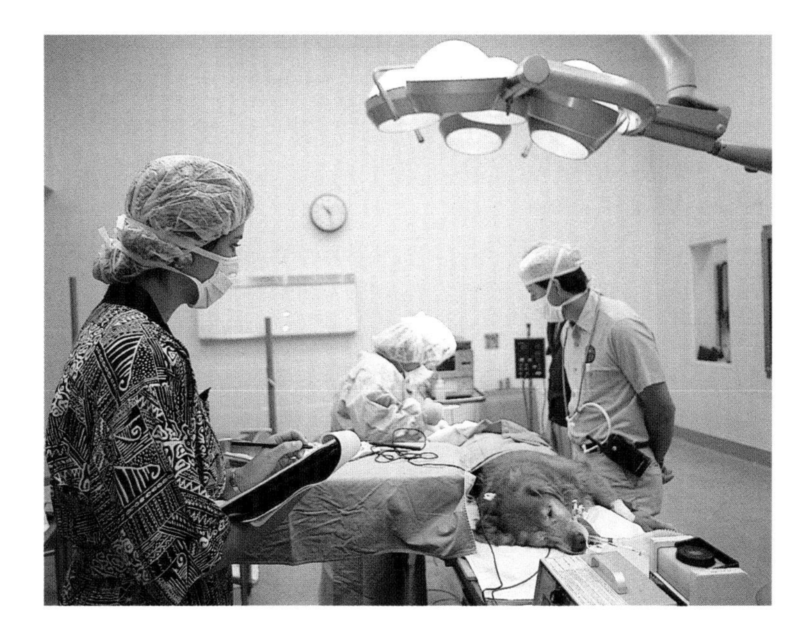

him constantly. He searched an indoor sleeping area where he and Anna spent most of their nights together. He chirped his distress, but Anna wasn't coming back.

Kathy decided that it wasn't a good idea to introduce Arusha to a new dog friend because he was old and set in his ways. With his big size and strength, Arusha might hurt a dog that he was unfamiliar with.

To keep Arusha occupied, the trainers took him for many walks. Without Anna as his security blanket, though, he was more skittish during those walks. Kathy also moved Arusha to a variety of empty animal pens throughout the day. Each pen had new sights and smells for Arusha to explore.

Gradually, Arusha grew accustomed to life without Anna. He began appearing at special events and school assemblies again, and debuted in the Wild Ones show. Arusha, with Kathy's help, even became an animal artist by walking through colorful paint and onto a canvas. The pawprint painting was sold at an art auction to raise money for wildlife conservation.

Kathy is still sad when she thinks of Arusha without his beloved Anna. But in Kathy's heart, Arusha the cheetah and Anna the dog will be forever friends.

### LOUNGING LIONS

**COMMON NAME:** Lion

**SCIENTIFIC NAME:** *Panthera leo*

**NICKNAME:** The King of Beasts

**FOUND IN:** Much of Africa; the Gir Forest in India.

**HABITAT:** Grassy plains, savannahs, deserts, open woodlands.

**SIZE:** Males: 330–550 pounds, four feet tall at shoulder. Females: 260–400 pounds, three-and-a-half feet tall at shoulder.

**LIFESTYLE:** Most social of the big cats. Lives in family groups called prides. Prides can be two to forty lions, mostly females (lionesses) and cubs; average size is fifteen. Males defend prides' territory.

**OFFSPRING:** Female lion has a litter of one to six cubs about every two years. Cub birth weight: three pounds.

African lion

**FEEDING HABITS:** Carnivorous (meat-eater). Eats mainly wildebeests, giraffes, zebras, warthogs, buffalos, impalas, and other antelopes. Hunts by stalking, then rushes and leaps on prey. Females do most of hunting; sometimes in groups. Males in prides eat first.

**Lifespan:** Ten to twelve years in the wild; up to thirty years in captivity.

**Wild status:** Asian lions are critically endangered due to hunting and habitat loss. African lion population is dwindling for same reasons, but not in danger of extinction yet.

**Special facts:** Rests up to twenty-one hours a day. Active mainly at dawn, dusk, or night. Adult males have manes. Excellent sense of sight, hearing, and smell. Roars can be heard five miles away.

**Persian leopards**

## ADAPTABLE LEOPARDS

**Common name:** Leopard

**Scientific name:** *Panthera pardus*

**Nickname:** Panther

**Found in:** Much of Africa; parts of the Middle East and Asia including China, India, Southeast Asia, Siberia, Arabian Peninsula.

**Habitat:** Deserts, grasslands, forests, mountains, bush country.

**Size:** Males: 80–200 pounds, 18–32 inches tall at shoulder. Females: 60–130 pounds, 18–32 inches tall at shoulder.

**Lifestyle:** Mostly solitary. Lives in territories. A male's territory usually overlaps the territory of one or two females. Males fight to keep other males out of their area.

**Offspring:** Female leopard has litter of one to six cubs every one or two years. Cubs are born in a cave, hollow tree, or thicket. Cub birth weight: fifteen to twenty ounces.

**Feeding habits:** Carnivorous. Eats prey including gazelles, impalas, wildebeests, deer, wild goats, monkeys, pigs. Hunts by stalking and ambushing. Often bites throat of big victims and strangles them. Can carry heavy carcasses into trees to store them.

**Lifespan:** Up to twelve years in the wild; more than twenty in captivity.

**Wild status:** Endangered due to hunting for fur and trophies, loss of habitat.

**Special facts:** Extremely strong. Good tree climbers. Most adaptable big cat. Can live in almost any habitat. Spotted coats including black spots on black or tan fur. All black is a color phase, not a separate species. Spots help leopard blend in with surroundings. Mainly nocturnal. Can roar.

## SECRETIVE JAGUARS

**Common name:** Jaguar

**Scientific name:** *Panthera onca*

**Nickname:** El Tigre

**Found in:** Mexico, Central and South America.

**Habitat:** Mainly dense forests near rivers, lakes, swamps; sometimes grasslands or bushy areas near water.

**Size:** Males: 200–300 pounds, 27–30 inches tall at shoulder. Females: 160–240 pounds, 22–24 inches tall at shoulder.

**Lifestyle:** Mainly solitary. Lives in territories. Marks territory by spraying urine and clawing trees.

**Brazilian jaguar**

**Offspring:** Litter of one to four cubs is born in a den. Cub birth weight: twenty-four to thirty-two ounces. Young live with mother for two years.

**Feeding habits:** Carnivorous. Eats almost anything that's available—deer, snakes, lizards, peccaries, capybaras, turtles, monkeys, cattle.

Hunts alone, mostly on the ground, both day and night. Stalks, then ambushes prey. Will drag prey long distances to sheltered spot. Kills large prey by biting its head.

**LIFESPAN:** Up to twenty-two years in captivity.

**WILD STATUS:** Endangered due to hunting for fur, also hunted by cattle ranchers; habitat loss.

**SPECIAL FACTS:** Stocky and the most powerful of the American cats. Swims and climbs well. Elusive, secretive, difficult for scientists to study in the wild. Spotted coat, including black spots on black or yellowish tan fur. Can roar but usually grunts, snarls, growls.

African cheetah

## SPEEDING CHEETAHS

**COMMON NAME:** Cheetah

**SCIENTIFIC NAME:** *Acinonyx jubatus*

**NICKNAME:** Fastest land mammal on Earth

**FOUND IN:** Africa except Sahara desert and tropical forests in central Africa; small area in Middle East, mainly Iran.

**HABITAT:** Open grasslands, semi-desert, thick bush.

**SIZE:** Males and females: 80–150 pounds, 27–35 inches tall at shoulder.

**LIFESTYLE:** Live in home ranges alone or sometimes in small groups. Groups are usually females with cubs, or several related males.

**OFFSPRING:** Litter of one to eight cubs born every seventeen to twenty months. Mother hides cubs in grass, thick bush; moves them almost daily. Cub birth weight: six to eleven ounces.

**FEEDING HABITS:** Carnivorous. Eats gazelles, wildebeests, impalas, hares. Hunts during the day. Stalks prey and then charges at top speed, up to seventy-miles per hour for a few hundred yards. Knocks prey down with its force, then grabs throat and strangles. Most hunts fail.

**LIFESPAN:** Up to twelve years in the wild; up to nineteen years in captivity.

**WILD STATUS:** Endangered due to habitat loss and hunting for fur.

**SPECIAL FACTS:** Built for speed. Slim, muscular body; small head; long legs. Non-retractable claws (like dogs' claws) for traction when sprinting. Spotted coat with black "tear stripes" running from eyes to mouth. Purrs but can't roar. People have tamed cheetahs and used them to hunt game for 4,300 years.

## MIGHTY TIGERS

**COMMON NAME:** Tiger

**SCIENTIFIC NAME:** *Panthera tigris*

**NICKNAME:** The King of Beasts (in Asia)

**FOUND IN:** Asia including India, China, Indonesia, Russia, Southeast Asia.

**HABITAT:** Tropical rainforests, snow-covered taiga, mangrove swamps, evergreen forests, grasslands, rocky country. Must have good cover, water, and plenty of large prey.

**SIZE:** Varies among subspecies. Siberian tigers—males: 400–700 pounds; females: 220–370 pounds. Other subspecies—males: 200–560 pounds; females: 140–350 pounds.

**LIFESTYLE:** Usually solitary. Females (tigresses) spend a large part of life with dependent youngsters. Live in territories but are generally friendly with other tigers who have overlapping ranges.

**OFFSPRING:** Litter of one to six cubs born every two to two-and-a-half years. Cub birth weight: two to three pounds. Young live with mother for two to three years. Half of all wild tiger cubs die before two years of age.

**FEEDING HABITS:** Carnivorous. Eats large prey including deer, antelopes, buffaloes, pigs, gaur, sometimes humans. Searches for prey, sneaks up on it and gets as close as possible by hiding behind

**Sumatran tiger**

cover such as rocks, bushes, and trees; leaps at prey and ambushes it by grabbing throat or nape of neck, dislocates the vertebrae. Drags prey to dense cover. Can eat up to ninety pounds of meat in one sitting. Only one in ten hunts is successful.

**LIFESPAN:** Usually fifteen to twenty years in the wild and captivity, but sometimes up to twenty-six years.

**WILD STATUS:** Endangered due to hunting for fur, trophies, and body parts used in native medicine; loss of habitat. Also killed when they're a threat to humans.

**SPECIAL FACTS:** Largest cat. Rests during the day, active at dusk, night. All are striped, but stripe pattern varies. Most are orange or yellow and black. A few are white with dark stripes because of a recessive gene. Exceptionally strong and powerful. Good swimmers and will lounge in water. Can roar.

**Sumatran tiger**

# BIBLIOGRAPHY


Clutton-Brock, Juliet. *Cat*. Eyewitness Books series. New York: Alfred A. Knopf, 1991.

Green, Richard. *Wild Cat Species of the World*. Plymouth, England: Basset Publications, 1991.

Lavine, Sigmund A. *Wonders of Tigers*. New York: Dodd, Mead & Company, Inc., 1987.

Lumpkin, Dr. Susan. *Big Cats: Great Creatures of the World*. New York: Facts On File, Inc., 1993.

Neff, Nancy A. *The Big Cats: The Paintings of Guy Coheleach*. New York: Harry N. Abrams, Inc., 1982.

Ricciuti, Edward R. *The Wild Cats*. New York: The Ridge Press, Inc., and Newsweek, Inc., 1979.

Ryden, Hope. *Your Cat's Wild Cousins*. New York: Lodestar Books, 1991.

Seidensticker, Dr. John, and Dr. Susan Lumpkin, eds. *Great Cats: Majestic Creatures of the Wild*. Emmaus, PA: Rodale Press, Inc., 1991.

Thapar, Valmik. *Tiger: Portrait of a Predator*. New York: Facts On File, Inc., 1986.

Wexo, John Bonnett. *Big Cats*. Zoobooks series. San Diego: Wildlife Education, Ltd., 1992.


**VIDEOS**


*Land of the Tiger*, produced by The National Geographic Society and WQED/Pittsburgh, 1985. 60 minutes. These cats are shown hunting, playing, fighting, and caring for their young.

*Lions of the African Night*, produced by The National Geographic Society and WQED/Pittsburgh, 1987. 60 minutes. A pride of lions is tracked as they search for prey in the bush.

*Season of the Cheetah*, a National Geographic Video produced by Wildlife Film Productions, 1989. 60 minutes. A family of cheetahs competes with abundant wildlife for food in the Serengeti Plain.

*The Secret Leopard*, a National Geographic Video produced by Zebra Films, 1986. 60 minutes. An in-depth look at the habits of the camouflaged, elusive hunter.